THE
PURPLE TURKEY

and
Other Thanksgiving Riddles

THE
PURPLE TURKEY
and
Other Thanksgiving Riddles

David A. Adler

illustrated by

Marylin Hafner

Holiday House / New York

To my nephew, Jonathan
D.A.A.

For my brother, Everett
M.H.

Text copyright © 1986 by David A. Adler
Illustrations copyright © 1986 by Marylin Hafner
All rights reserved
Printed in the United States of America

Library of Congress Cataloging-in-Publication Data

Adler, David A.
The purple turkey and other Thanksgiving riddles.

SUMMARY: An illustrated collection of humorous
riddles on a Thanksgiving Day theme.
1. Riddles, Juvenile. 1. Thanksgiving Day—Wit and
humor. [1. Riddles. 2. Thanksgiving Day—Wit and humor.
3. Wit and humor] I. Hafner, Marylin, ill. II. Title.
PN6371.5.A3227 1986   818'.5402   86-310
ISBN 0-8234-0613-X

What's purple and covered with feathers?

A turkey holding its breath.

What has fur on the outside and feathers on the inside?

A turkey in a raccoon coat.

What's the key to a good Thanksgiving Day dinner?

Turkey.

What do you get if you cross a turkey with a porcupine?

Splinters in your drumsticks.

If April showers bring May flowers, what do May flowers bring?

Pilgrims.

What has feathers and runs to the dinner table?

One dumb turkey.

Why are the Pilgrims buried in Massachusetts?

Because they're dead.

When did the Pilgrims first say "God bless America?"

The first time they heard America sneeze.

What do you get when you cross a canary with a turkey?

A peeping Tom.

Why did the cranberry sauce blush?

It saw the salad dressing.

What did one baby ear of corn say to the other?

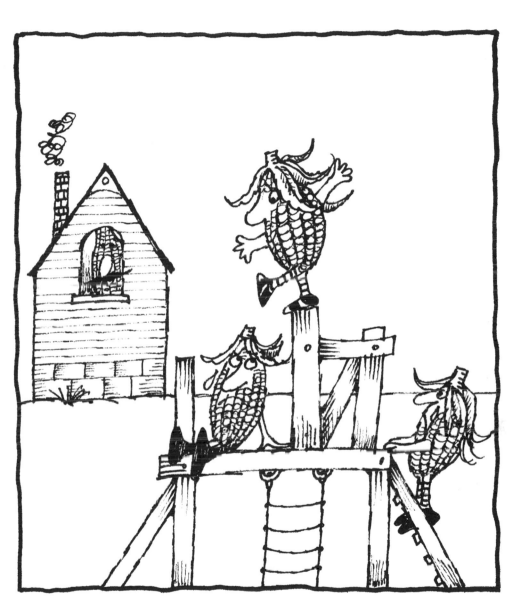

Where's pop corn?

What do you get when you cross a turkey with a centipede?

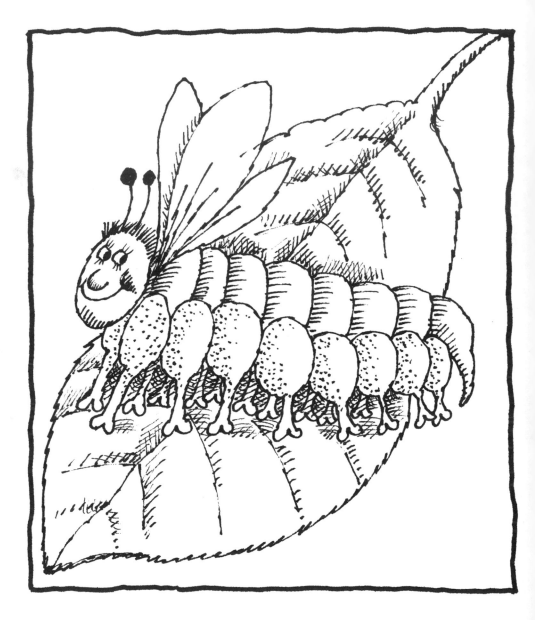

Lots of drumsticks.

Why was Tom Turkey thrown out of school?

He used foul (fowl) language.

What happened to the turkey after it fell into the wine sauce?

It gobbled and wobbled.

What would you call a pet squash?

Call it anything you want. It won't hear you.

Why can't you freeze cranberry juice?

Those little berries just don't concentrate.

What did the Pilgrim say to the green pumpkin?

"Why orange you orange?"

What gobbles, has feathers and sixteen wheels?

A turkey on roller skates.

What's the best way to keep a turkey from charging?

Take away its credit cards.

When the Pilgrims landed, where did they stand?

On their feet.

Why did the turkey cross the road?

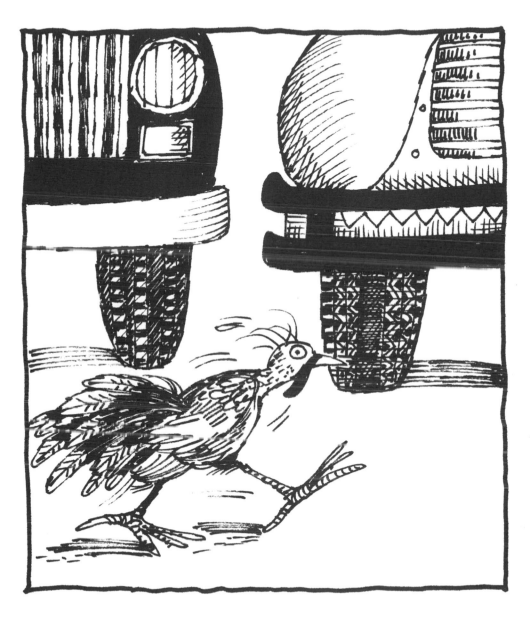

It was the chicken's day off.

Why did the farmer put suntan lotion on his turkey?

He liked dark meat.

How long is a pair of moccasins?

Two feet.

Which Indians are the best flycatchers?

The Cleveland Indians.

Which side is the left side of a pumpkin pie?

The side you haven't eaten.

What has one feather, two eyes, and three ears?

An Indian eating corn.

Why did the Indians whisper?

The corn had ears.

How is a turkey sitting on a fence just like a dime?

Its head is on one side, and its tail is on the other.

Why didn't Tom Turkey eat dessert?

He was stuffed.

Where does corn come from?

The stalk brings it.

What did the cranberry vine say to the farmer?

"Stop picking on me."

What's the best thing to put into a pumpkin pie?

Your teeth.

What do turkeys learn in first-aid class?

Beak-to-beak resuscitation.

I saw a turkey egg that's bigger than an elephant. Can you beat that?

Sure. With an eggbeater.

What's the best way to catch a turkey?

Sneak up on a turkey egg and wait.

How many turkeys would you need to serve twenty-four?

Turkeys aren't very good at serving. You'd be better off with a waiter or waitress.

What should you know before you teach tricks to a turkey?

More than the turkey.

What has feathers, bubbles, and spins?

A turkey in the wash.

What would you get if you crossed an octopus with a turkey?

Eight feather dusters.

What would the Pilgrims be growing if they plowed all morning and planted all afternoon?

Tired.

What are unhappy cranberries called?

Blueberries.

What's round, red, and wears a diaper?

A baby cranberry.

How can you get a turkey to fly?

Buy it an airplane ticket.

Why did the Indian yell?

Someone was stepping on his corn.

Should you drink cranberry juice after a bath?

You can drink the juice, but I don't think
you should drink the bath.

Why did Pilgrim leader Miles Standish go down in history?

He didn't do his homework.

Where should a turkey go if it loses its tail?

To the retail store.

What smells the best at a Thanksgiving Day dinner?

Your nose.

What does a corn doctor cure?

Earaches.

Which Pilgrim giggled on the Mayflower?

Miles Ticklish.

Why is an ear of corn like the British army?

It's full of kernels.

Why did the turkey sit on the tomahawk?

To hatchet.

What did the leftover drumstick say to the cranberry sauce?

"Foiled again."

How did Polly Pilgrim feel about making her own clothes?

Sew-sew.

What does Miles Standish do when he's tired?

He sitish.

What should you give a seasick Pilgrim?

A place by the rail.

Why are baby turkeys so dizzy when they come out of the egg?

They have shell shock.

Can you cook a turkey dinner in your pajamas?

Yes, but sometimes the gravy leaks out the sleeves.

How do you make squash salad?

Take lettuce and tomatoes and jump on them.

Why is expensive corn like a pirate?

Because it's a buccaneer.

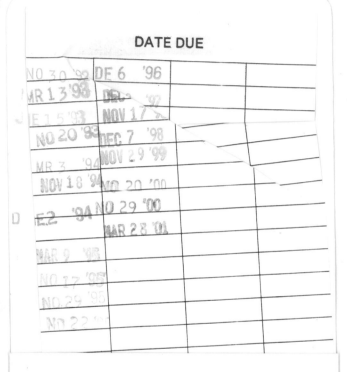